GRUMBLERUG'S GANG
The Day the Mums Disappeared

Karen Wallace
Illustrated by Kim Blundell

Collins
An Imprint of HarperCollinsPublishers

First published in Great Britain by
CollinsChildren'sBooks 1996

3 5 7 9 8 6 4 2

CollinsChildren'sBooks is a division of
HarperCollins*Publishers* Ltd,
77-85 Fulham Palace Road,
Hammersmith, London W6 8JB

Printed and bound in Great Britain by
Caledonian International Book Manufacturing Ltd, Glasgow

ISBN Hardback 0 00 185631 6
Paperback 0 00 675139 3

Chapter One

A long, long time ago, in a cave in the mountains, there lived a great big hairy bear-rug called Grumblerug.

Grumblerug shared his cave with
Mr and Mrs Blockhead and their
children Chips and Rocky.

Mr and Mrs Ribcage and *their*
children Billy, Tilly and Little Millie
lived there too.

Grumblerug was so big that all the children could sit on him at the same time. He grumbled about their muddy feet and the crumbs they dropped. But he didn't really mind because Grumblerug liked to feel part of the family.

One day, Little Millie had a brilliant idea. She whispered in Grumblerug's ear.

"Can we call ourselves Grumblerug's Gang, please?"

"Humph," grumbled Grumblerug, who wasn't called Grumblerug for nothing.

"You already make such a mess with your muddy feet and your crumbs. Humph, I suppose I wouldn't mind, too much. Humph! All right, then."

Secretly, of course, Grumblerug loved the idea. Grumblerug's Gang made him feel important. Grumblerug's Gang made him almost – SMILE!

Chapter Two

The next day, Rocky Blockhead called a top secret emergency meeting of Grumblerug's Gang. "It's almost Mothers' Day," he announced. "What are we going to give our mums?"

"I dunno," said Little Millie Ribcage.

"I dunno," said Chips Blockhead.

"How about a nice rock?" suggested Billy Ribcage.

His sister Tilly shook her head. "Our mum's got lots of rocks already," she said. "We have to think of something *special*."

"How about a *special* rock?" said Little Millie.

"Ssh!" said her sister.

"What about a new tooth necklace?" suggested Billy. "Mum's old one went into the soup pot last week."

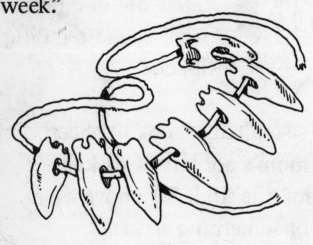

"That's a good idea," said Little
Millie, licking her lips. "I like soup."
Tilly Ribcage rolled her eyes. "A
new necklace isn't for the soup pot,"
she said. "It's for Mum to wear."

"Let's go hunting!" cried Chips. "Then Rocky and I could make a fur hat for *our* Mum and you could make a brand new tooth necklace for *yours!*"

"It's too late to go hunting," muttered Grumblerug. "Mothers' Day is tomorrow. Why don't you brush me instead?"

Billy patted Grumblerug's head. "Clever Grumblerug," he said. "I bet *you* know how we could do something in time."

"Humph," muttered Grumblerug.

"Nice Grumblerug," said Tilly, tickling his ears. "There must be *some* way."

"Humph," muttered Grumblerug, who liked having his ears tickled better than anything in the world. "Well, I suppose—"

"Suppose what?" asked Little Millie, her eyes wide.

"Humph," muttered Grumblerug again, "I suppose you could dig a pit and put vines and sticks over it. But you must—"

"That's a brilliant idea!" cried Chips, jumping up and grabbing his bone shovel. And before Grumblerug could finish his sentence, all the children had run off and he was covered in dust.

Chapter Three

The children ran across the field and along a narrow path. They came to a clearing in the middle of the woods. The grass was soft and green. The sun was warm and all around there were lots of blackberry bushes.

"This looks like a good place for the pit," said Chips.

"Why?" said Billy.

"It's just beside the blackberry bushes," said Chips. "An animal will wander into the clearing, eat lots and lots of berries, feel sleepy in the sunshine and—"

"It won't even notice falling into our pit!" cried Little Millie, jumping up and down.

"Exactly," said Chips, feeling very pleased with himself.

"It's a good idea," said Billy in a serious voice. "But we'll need to dig a very deep pit."

"I've brought some cold lizard and leaf sandwiches," said Rocky. "They'll make us feel strong."

"Ugh," said Little Millie. "They won't make *me* feel strong. I hate cold lizard and leaf sandwiches."

"So do I," said Tilly.

"We'll get some vines and sticks to cover the top, just as Grumblerug told us," said Little Millie.

"But what about your lunch?"
said Chips.

"We'll find something," said Little
Millie. She had seen an even *bigger*
blackberry bush on their way
through the woods. She put both
sandwiches in her pocket and
walked with Tilly out of the
clearing.

Chapter Four

When they had finished *their* sandwiches, Chips, Rocky and Billy picked up their bone shovels and started to dig.

The ground was soft and soon lumps of earth were flying through the air, landing in a heap on the side. Then after a while the lumps of earth stopped appearing out of the pit.

Chips, Rocky and Billy had been
having such a good time, they had
dug the pit too deep. Now they
couldn't get out of it.

When Tilly and Little Millie
returned, the clearing was empty.

"Where are the boys?" cried Little
Millie.

"Down here," shouted Chips,
Rocky and Billy. "We're stuck!"

"What are we going to do?" cried Little Millie, her eyes as big as saucers.

Tilly looked at the vines she was carrying. "We'll tie one of these vines to a tree," she said. "Then we'll drop the other end down into the pit."

But it wasn't as easy as that.
The first vine was too short.

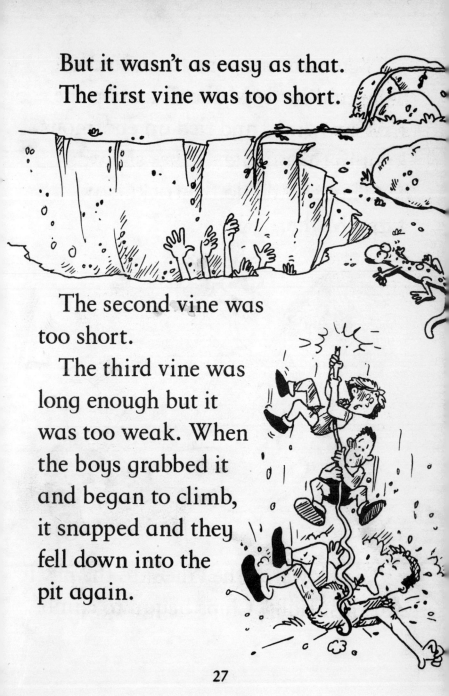

The second vine was too short.

The third vine was long enough but it was too weak. When the boys grabbed it and began to climb, it snapped and they fell down into the pit again.

There was only one thing to do. Tilly and Little Millie picked up the first two vines and tied an enormous knot in the middle.

"That should do the trick," said Little Millie.

They lowered the vine into the pit. It was just right. Chips began to climb.

When Rocky, Billy and Chips finally climbed out, they were covered in dirt and looked like three moles.

Tilly and Little Millie filled the bottom of the pit with leaves. Then they spread vines and branches across the top. They were covered with twigs and sticks.

They looked like two hedgehogs!

"What are we going to do?" said Chips. "Our mum's a rhino if we get our clothes messy."

"Our mum's a Tyrannosaurus Rex," said Little Millie.

"Let's wash our clothes in the waterfall just like the mums do," said Rocky.

"Isn't washing clothes rather hard work?" asked Chips.

"The mums do it all the time," said Billy.

Little Millie thought hard for a minute. Chips was right. Washing clothes was hard work. "We'll swim round and round in the pool," she said. "That way the muddy bits will drop off!"

Chapter Five

Chips, Rocky, Tilly, Billy and Little Millie played in the waterfall for the rest of the day.

They jumped off the rock.

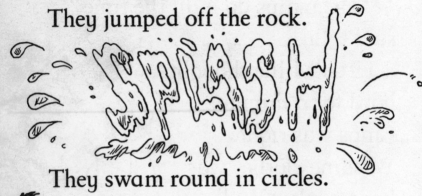

They swam round in circles.

They splashed and shouted and jumped and twirled.

They forgot all about washing
their clothes properly but most of the
muddy bits dropped off anyway.

The sun was going down behind
the mountain when the children set
off back to their cave.

"I'm starving," said Tilly. "I
wonder what the mums have made
for supper."

"I wonder what they've made for pudding," said Little Millie.

"It's my turn scraping the bowl," said Rocky.

"It's my turn nearest the fire," said Chips.

But when they got home, the cave was empty. Nobody was there.

"Look!" cried Chips. "There's a message on the wall!"

Mr Ribcage was a cave painter and decorator. He had painted a picture message on the wall. The children looked at it carefully.

"The dads have gone hunting," read Chips slowly. "There's a gigantic egg for supper on the ledge." He turned to the others. "What do you do with a gigantic egg?" he asked.

"Build a fire and make a big omelette," muttered Grumblerug.

Everyone groaned.

Nobody knew how to make a big omelette. Nobody knew how to build a fire. The mums always did that.

"I'm cold," whined Billy.

"I'm hungry," said Rocky.

"Where are the mums?" asked Little Millie.

"They can't have gone far," said Tilly. "They'll be back soon."

"When?" asked Little Millie. But nobody knew. So Billy, Tilly, Rocky and Chips ate the cold lizard and green leaf sandwiches that Little Millie had stuffed into her pocket.

Even Little Millie had a couple of bites. She pretended they were pieces of cake left over from her birthday.

"Who's going to tell us a story?" asked Chips.

Nobody spoke.

The mums always did that too.

Little Millie looked at Grumblerug but Grumblerug had closed his eyes and was snoring loudly.

There was nothing else to do.

The children curled up beside Grumblerug and went to sleep as well.

That night they all dreamed the same dream.

They dreamed of the big hot breakfast their mums would make them in the morning.

Chapter Six

The next day was Mothers' Day but when the children woke up, the cave was still cold and empty.

"Do you think the mums have been swallowed by that greedyguts swamp monster?" asked Rocky.

Chips shook his head. "He only likes crocodiles and lily pads," he said. "Anyway the mums never go near the swamp since they slipped on the mud and got all slimy."

"I like getting slimy," said Little Millie.

"The mums don't," said Chips.

"Do you think they've been carried away by the huge skinny bird with the curved beak that blots out the sun when he lands on his nest?" asked Tilly.

Chips shook his head. "The huge skinny bird only eats toads and frogs," he said. "Anyway you can see his nest from the cave. The mums would wave if they were there."

"Maybe the mums have been kidnapped by a tribe of ferocious hunters!" cried Billy. "And carried off into a secret hideaway in the mountains!"

Chips shook his head. "Nobody could make the mums do something they didn't want to do," he said firmly.

Everybody thought about this for a moment.

Chips was right.

But that still didn't solve the problem.

"I'm cold," muttered Rocky.

"I'm hungry," whined Tilly.

"Where's my breakfast?" grumbled Grumblerug.

"Do you think," said Little Millie, "that the mums are hiding up a tree because they are fed up with washing clothes, making fires and cooking meals?"

"Never!" said Chips and Rocky firmly.

Billy and Tilly shook their heads. "Impossible!" they said.

"What do *you* think, Grumblerug," said Little Millie.

"Humph," said Grumblerug, as if he should have been asked in the first place. "Last time I saw your mums they were planning to pick berries in the clearing in the wood and they *promised* to bring some back for my supper."

The children stared at him with their mouths hanging open.

"The mums were going to the clearing?" cried Billy.

"The clearing in the woods?" repeated Rocky.

"Why didn't you tell us?" shouted Chips.

"I tried to," grumbled Grumblerug. "You wouldn't listen. You ran off and—"

But he never finished his sentence because the children had run off and once again he was covered in dust.

Chapter Seven

"Chips," said Tilly as they raced across the field towards the wood. "Are you thinking what I'm thinking?"

"If it's what *we're* thinking," said Rocky. "Then we're all thinking the same thing!"

"Oh no!" cried Little Millie. "Do you think there'll be *any* berries left for us?"

"Millie!" said her sister in a sharp voice. "That's not what we were thinking at all!"

"Ssh!" said Rocky.

At the edge of clearing where the grass was soft and green, the sound of voices laughing and talking floated up into the sunshine.

Chips and Billy suddenly stopped. The others only just managed not to bump into them.

Billy held his finger to his lips. The children stood as still as statues. They listened to the voices that seemed to be coming out of the ground.

"Of course, I always knew she'd choose one of those itchy, hairy dresses," said the first voice with a giggle. "No one wears leather, these days."

"And as for the snake-skin bag," said the second voice. There was a hoot of laughter.

"It's the mums!" whispered Little Millie her eyes as big as soup plates. "They fell into our pit!"

"Quick!" cried Tilly. "Where are the vines we tied together?"

"Here!" cried Chips, tying one end to a tree and dragging the other to the side of the pit.

"Mum!" yelled Billy Ribcage.

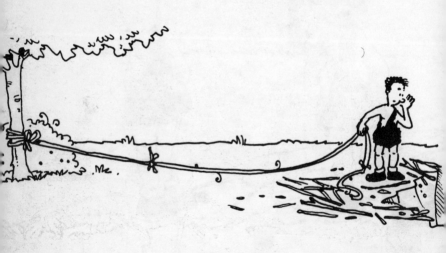

"Mum!" yelled Rocky Blockhead.

They pulled away what was left of the twigs and peered over the edge.

Chapter Eight

Mrs Blockhead was leaning against the earth wall at the bottom of the pit. Her legs were stretched out in front of her. Mrs Ribcage was lying on her side propped up by one elbow.

Both mums looked up and blinked in the sunlight. But neither of them seem at all worried.

"We've come to rescue you!" cried Little Millie.

"Have you?" said Mrs Blockhead. She sounded almost disappointed.

"We've had such a *wonderful* time," said Mrs Ribcage, sitting up and stretching her arms. "We were picking berries and we fell into this lovely soft pit."

"We've been eating and chatting ever since," said Mrs Blockhead. "No cooking or washing or building fires for a whole day."

"It's been just like a holiday," said Mrs Ribcage.

"We dug the pit for Mothers' Day," cried Little Millie, clapping her hands.

"Did you really?" cried Mrs Blockhead. "What a brilliant idea."

"Yes!" said Little Millie, taking a deep breath. "We wanted to—"

"Do something *special* for you," said Billy, quickly putting his hand over his sister's mouth.

Mrs Blockhead and Mrs Ribcage stood up and dusted off their clothes.

"It *was* special," said Mrs Blockhead, smiling.

"The best Mothers' Day present ever," agreed Mrs Ribcage. Then slowly they took hold of the vine and climbed out of the pit.

They all walked along the narrow
path through the woods.

When they reached the field a low
rumbling filled the air. It sounded
like the beginning of
a thunderstorm.

"Goodness!" cried Mrs Ribcage.
"We'd better hurry. It sounds like
rain."

Chips, Rocky, Billy, Tilly and
Little Millie raced across the field as
fast as they could. They weren't
running because of the rain.

They knew it wasn't going to rain. The low rumbling was the sound of empty stomachs - *their* empty stomachs!

On the other side of field, smoke was curling into the sky. Smoke meant fire, and fire meant FOOD!

Back at the cave, Mr Blockhead and Mr Ribcage had returned from their hunting trip and had built an enormous fire.

"Mothers' Day Lunch!" they called. "Mammoth burgers and berry pie!"

Mr Ribcage held out two parcels. "Here's something special for the mums," he said.

Mrs Ribcage and Mrs Blockhead opened their presents.

The children could hardly believe their eyes.

There was a soft fur hat for Mrs Blockhead.

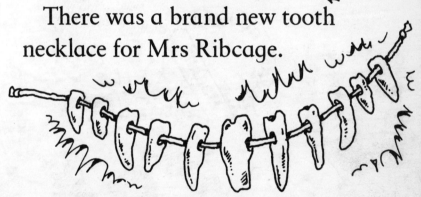

There was a brand new tooth necklace for Mrs Ribcage.

"And I have a surprise too," said Mr Ribcage. He led them inside the cave. The walls were covered in paintings!

"Grumblerug told me everything,"
said Mr Ribcage. "So I decided to
paint the whole story as a very
special Mothers' Day present."

A huge grin spread across his
face. "It's called *Grumblerug's
Gang and The Day the Mums
Disappeared!*"